Sobaka
Finds a Home

BECKY WILLIAMS

authorHOUSE®

AuthorHouse™
1663 Liberty Drive
Bloomington, IN 47403
www.authorhouse.com
Phone: 1 (800) 839-8640

Published by AuthorHouse   10/18/2016

ISBN: 978-1-5246-4464-2 (sc)
ISBN: 978-1-5246-4463-5 (e)

Library of Congress Control Number: 2016916845

Print information available on the last page.

Any people depicted in stock imagery provided by Thinkstock are models, and such images are being used for illustrative purposes only. Certain stock imagery © Thinkstock.

This book is printed on acid-free paper.

CONTENTS

CHAPTER 1

My Birth

For a dog, I guess I have had a good life. It's hard to know for sure because my life is the only one I know firsthand. Yes, after thinking about it further, I can say I have had a *good* life! I guess if I would have chosen where to live my life, it might have been somewhere besides the plains of Texas. Then again, Texas is not so bad. The weather is mild, and the food is good (when I can get people food). And regardless how I felt about it, I entered this world in Lubbock, Texas.

My birthday was like any other, I suppose. I was born in a doghouse behind the main house to a beautiful white Maltese on April 10, 2008. Mom was the queen of her castle, and she loved having her puppies.

When I first entered the world, I could not see or hear, but it wasn't long until I had full awareness of my surroundings, which included sight, sound, smell, and touch. I discovered a new life with the warmth of my mother and the joy of exploring my new world. I could feel the goodness of God my creator, as He had blessed me with a home and love and all the fresh new experiences of a newborn puppy—which included two sisters!

My sisters didn't look anything like me. They were both fluffy and white like a full Maltese. My fur was anything but fluffy. It was medium length, thin, and wild. I was slightly bigger than my sisters, and with my different looks, I immediately fell into the role of taking charge in my small family. At least as much as Mom would let me.

Mom made sure we stayed in the doghouse until she thought we could run and see well enough to escape trouble. If I tried to wander too far, she would pick me up with her teeth, ever gently, and take me back to the safety of the doghouse. Although I was curious about my world, Mom knew it was not safe.

Mom's human family was very nice. They pretty much left us puppies to grow up under Mom's watchful eye. A few times a day, they would come into the yard, give Mom food and water, and play ball. I found out they called Mom "Sassy." That was a pretty name for a Maltese. They did not have a name for us three puppies.

The humans were used to Sassy having puppies. This was her fifth litter, and selling Maltese puppies was a nice income for the human family. Maltese dogs were in high demand,

and I can see why. Their white thick coats are just beautiful. Sassy liked having puppies, and her human family loved her.

Sassy explained to us how things worked in the dog-human world. She explained that God created domesticated dogs to love humans and to help humans with a job.

"I have a good human family," Sassy explained. "They give me food and water. They groom me by giving me a bath and brushing my fur. They play ball with me and hug me whenever they get a chance.

"All domesticated dogs are created by God to be loyal and true to the humans in their world," Sassy continued. "Dogs are happiest in the human world when they have a job to do to help the humans in their world."

"Why do dogs have to help humans?" I asked.

"God created dogs with instincts, which are internal desires and knowledge that come naturally. Now as a small puppy, your instinct is to stay with me, drink my milk, and listen to my wise instruction. But as you grow, you will become anxious to see the rest of the world. You will start to have a desire to leave this backyard and start a new life with a human family and a job of your own."

I really had to think hard about that statement.

I overheard Sassy's human family one day talking about my "look." They were not exactly thrilled by it. I heard them say, "This puppy does not look like a Maltese. It looks like the terrier next door but with longer fur. We may have trouble finding a home for her."

I didn't understand this. What did "trouble finding a home" mean? I had to ask Sassy.

"It's hard to explain," Sassy said, "but I will try. I am a Maltese. We are great human pets because as a breed we are gentle and well-mannered.

"Terriers, on the other hand, are high-energy dogs that love active dog jobs. This doesn't mean that Maltese are better than terriers, just that they are different.

"You are different from your sisters because your father is the terrier that lives next door. So you are part Maltese and part terrier. Your fur and markings are just what God ordered them to be. You are different, and you are valuable.

"You will make some human family a perfect dog someday. The trouble is finding the right home. But don't you worry. God always has a plan."

As I quickly grew in strength and courage, I found out what a wonderful life puppies enjoy. Those first few weeks with Sassy were heaven. If I was hungry, Sassy quickly fed me. If I was sleepy, I just fell asleep anywhere—in the doghouse or out in the sun on the grass. If I wanted to play, I'd pester Sassy and my sisters. The backyard where we stayed was large enough that I could run, jump, and chase birds. I felt free. I did not worry about anything.

I did not know what lay outside our fence and into the yards beyond. I was curious to find out about the other creations God had in this universe, so I often stuck my head under our fence and looked beyond our yard.

I noticed there were other houses like ours with yards and streets. Every once in a while, a car would drive by, and it would scare me. At the time, I did not know about cars. I thought it must be a big animal that could run a lot faster than me. That gave me the idea that I should avoid cars if at all possible.

Other than cars, it looked great out there. But for now, Sassy made sure I stayed inside the yard.

After I had been in this world a few weeks, Sassy started making us puppies eat puppy food. It wasn't as good as Sassy's milk, but it smelled good and it was fun to chew the pieces of nugget. My new teeth were sharp and my jaw was strong, so chewing became my new pastime joy. I chewed on fences, gates, and everything else in our yard I could get my jaws around.

My human family wasn't thrilled with my chewing abilities, so they gave me a rawhide bone to chew. Boy, did it taste good!

My sisters tried to chew on my rawhide, but I was the boss of our yard and quickly yelped at them to get away. I guarded MY rawhide from them like it were lost treasure.

Over time, Sassy slowly became irritated with us for bothering her for milk. "It is time you puppies started eating more nugget puppy food and not just my milk," Sassy said. "If you ever want to grow up and become strong dogs, you need to eat solid food."

Slowly, we stopped drinking Sassy's milk and ate puppy food all the time.

When I was about two months old, I heard the human's talking that it was about time to find all the puppies a new human family.

"What did that mean?" I asked Sassy.

She explained, "God made dogs to be a help to the human world. Humans give you special treats and warm hugs. Humans provide you all the necessities of life—a place to live, water, food, and companionship.

"Dogs like us do not know how to hunt and provide our own food. We are small dogs and would be easy prey for chicken hawks or bigger dogs if it were not for the humans who keep us safe."

"You mean someday I am going to leave you and have a human family of my own?" I asked.

"Yes," she answered. "Remember what I taught you, and always be true to your instincts."

I then started to look forward to what my life might be like within the human world. I really wanted to see what the world was like beyond our yard. I just knew God had a perfect human family just for me.

CHAPTER

The New Family 2

One day, a strange human lady came into the backyard to look at us puppies. She had some dog treats and gave one to each of us. She picked each one of us up, held us in her arms, and immediately fell in love with … my sister! I knew I was different from my sisters, but I was hoping my looks would not matter when it came to finding me a human family. But the lady made it very clear that she wanted her new dog to look like a Maltese.

It wasn't long until my other sister was gone too. Then it was just Sassy and me. I missed my sisters and having someone to boss. I was anxious to be out on my own with my forever human family. Every time a visitor came to the backyard, I was sure this would be my new human family. But each time I was rejected. I felt so sad.

I was originally the leader of this puppy pack, and now I had no one to lead. I was supposed to be in charge! Why would any human pick the smaller dogs first? Wouldn't they like me best? My only option was to pray. "God, You know my desire is to be with a human family that will teach me to develop into a loyal, loving, hardworking dog. Please send a family to me I can call my own. Help me to be that special dog to a special human."

My day finally came when a big man came into the yard. He was taller than any other human I had ever seen, and his hands were rough when he reached down to pick me up. His face had a beard, so I couldn't tell if he was smiling or frowning.

"I have three boys at home," the man said. "They will love a puppy. They will not care if this puppy is a Maltese or a terrier. I think this one will fit in with my boys wonderfully!"

I was so excited! I was going to a human house that had human children! I could only imagine what fun I would have playing chase, eating treats, and seeing a world outside my now-lonely yard.

That would be my last day to be with Sassy. That may be sad in the human world, but in the dog world, it is a sign I was growing from a puppy to a dog. I was happy and scared at the same time. What an adventure I was going to have!

The man took me to his car. I had never ridden in a car before, and it scared me to death. I crouched down low to the seat and kept my tail tight underneath me.

I could feel the car move. I felt it go left, and then right, and then left. Every time the car turned, I would slide on the seat and bump my head. It seemed that the man was going real fast, but I could not tell for sure because no matter how hard I tried, I was not big enough to see out the windows.

I was excited about my new life, but something about the man seemed mean, and I wasn't sure if he really liked me or not. I really had nothing to base my fear on other than instinct. Something told me to beware.

When we arrived at my human family's house, three human boys came running to the car to greet me. They seemed very excited to have a puppy. I wagged my tail and greeted them back with a small bark. I was so proud of my new human family and very happy.

The man gathered me from the seat and took me into their house. I had never been inside a human house before, and it really scared me. It was darker inside than outside in the sun. It took a minute for my eyes to adjust.

There was lots of noise from the boys laughing and talking all at once, and it made me nervous. As soon as my human dad put me down, I ran under the nearest table to think about where I was.

I looked around. I was in a room that must have been a kitchen. It had a big bright rug with a table on it and several chairs around the table. There were lots of cabinets. I was as far under the table as I could go, trying to figure out my next move. I was really scared!

A lady came over and gave a look under the table. "Whose idea was it to bring home a puppy?" she said. "I don't want a puppy!" This didn't give me much comfort, but here I was!

Not knowing for sure what to do, I decided it might be best if I just stayed under the table and soaked in all the excitement. The humans kept talking about me, and after a short time, the youngest boy pulled me out to greet the family.

He was cute, about three years old, and I think he thought I was a ball because shortly after picking me up, he dropped me to the ground. I am so glad that I landed on my feet!

The first order of business for my new human family was to give me a name. They decided on Corkey. They showed me where my water bowl and food bowl was, and I quickly took a drink.

After I took a drink, the boys took me to their bedroom to play. There were three twin beds and lots of toys. This allowed me lots of places to explore and hide.

Later, the human mom came to the boys' bedroom and said, "It is time to take Corkey outside." The eldest boy was excited to pick me up and take me outside and show me their backyard.

Their backyard was bigger than my old one. It was full of tricycles, balls, and toys. I thought this yard held lots of adventure, and I looked forward to exploring my new surroundings.

After just a few minutes outside, the boys brought me back into the house. So began my outside/inside experience.

About every hour or so, someone was taking me outside and then back inside. I was going back and forth, inside and outside. It was confusing! I liked the inside of the house, and I liked the outside of the house. It seemed there was something my human family wanted me to learn, but I did not know what they were trying to teach me.

In time, I got the urge to go potty. The large colorful rug in the kitchen under the table came to mind. It looked nice and thick to me, so I decided it was a perfect spot, right in the middle the rug. As I started my business, the family started yelling, screaming, and jumping up. Someone grabbed me and threw me out the backdoor!

I was so confused. Did they not know I needed to go potty? In my old yard, no one ever told me I couldn't go potty wherever or whenever I wanted. Sassy would get mad and growl if I tried to "go" in the doghouse, but anywhere else was fine. Was it wrong to go potty in the house? I wouldn't think so. It must be okay because that nice, thick rug was perfect!

I soon learned that if I did something the family did not like, I got thrown outside. That didn't bother me so much because I liked being outside, but I also wanted to be with my humans. I wanted to find out what my job was and how I could help my human family. It was hard trying to understand this new world.

This cycle of being picked up and thrown outside continued. It seemed that this family did not understand dogs. And I sure did not understand them!

I was not with the family long before they decided I had to stay outside. I guess they didn't like me going potty on their rugs or chewing on anything within reach of my sharp teeth. I was trying real hard to please my human family, but I just couldn't understand what they expected.

For sure, the human dad did not like me around when he was home. If he saw me close, he'd give me a kick and I would go flying. I wanted to be his friend the most, but the kicks hurt and I thought it might be better to stay away.

The human mom was the one who gave me food and water. I was so happy for the daily food that I would jump and wag my tail, which made her upset. She would raise her voice and yell, "Get back!" I couldn't understand. I could tell by the tone of her voice that I was not supposed to be happy that she was giving me my food. Why did she not like me thanking her with my leaps of happiness?

I settled into a routine with my new human family. Pretty much, I stayed in their backyard by myself. The boys would come and play sometimes, but that scared me because they would pull my tail and hit me with their toys. I suppose they gave me hugs and loved me, but most of the time, I preferred being by myself.

This was my new life with my new human family. My reaction to them was based on my God-given instinct. No matter how they treated me, I would be a kind dog.

CHAPTER 3

The Storm

Lubbock is a great place for a dog to live outside because the weather is generally mild. It was spring when I went to live with my new family, so the birds were building nests, flowers were blooming, and grass was just starting to smell fresh and taste so good. But spring soon turned to summer, and the days got very hot!

This family did not have a doghouse like I had with Sassy. I explored to see what was in the yard that might provide me protection from the hot sun. There was a tree that provided shade and some shelter and a flower garden that seemed like a perfect place for me to potty. There was a chain link fence that I could see through, but there really wasn't much to see except more yards and more houses.

I tried to make the best of my new home. One day, I saw a bird in my yard and decided to chase the bird out of MY yard.

"Shoo, you bird!" I barked. "Get out of my yard! I am the boss here, and you cannot come in my yard without my permission!"

The bird looked at me and laughed. "Who do you think you are? You are a small dog, and I can fly to the heavens. I am faster than you. Watch me fly!"

Boy, did that make me mad! I decided right then and there that no bird would come close to my yard! Even though the bird could fly higher than I could jump, I discovered that birds had to land sometime, and they were not going to land in my yard!

My family didn't seem to notice my bird chasing, but it felt important to me. I was given a strong desire by God to have a job and help my humans. So I became a bird chaser.

Realizing that I was not getting a doghouse like I had with Sassy, I had to learn to exist without shelter from the wind, rain, or sunshine. If it was hot, I would lay on the grass and spread my legs out to cool off. If it was rainy, I learned to roll up in a ball and tuck my nose under my tail.

The first time it rained it seemed kind of fun to run around and feel the freshness. But soon, I would become cold because I had nowhere to go to dry my fur. I would shake off the moisture, but more rain would come. The ground I laid on was also wet and cold, and I thought my best option was to get under the tree and make the best of it. Rain usually didn't last long in Lubbock. I assured myself when I was wet and cold that the sun would shine soon and dry everything. It would be okay.

Rain made mud in my backyard. My fur was medium length and thin, which made it easy to matte into hard balls. I would lick the balls of fur and mud, but all that did was make them bigger and tighter. They became really uncomfortable.

Sassy's humans always brushed her fur. If she became muddy, they gave her a bath. I never thought I would like a brush or a bath, but now I wished a human would brush my fur. I guessed this human family did not own a brush.

One afternoon while I was exploring my yard, a big black cloud came over the house. The wind started blowing very hard, and I decided to take cover under my tree. I was afraid that if I stood up, the wind would blow me against the house, so I laid as flat as I could. Next, it started to rain. Not a gentle rain, but a big, blowing rain. The rain stung my skin and hurt my eyes. I was so afraid!

Shortly after the rain came a big bang followed by the brightest light I had ever seen!

I had experienced thunderstorms before with Sassy, but she made us stay in the nice, dry doghouse. Here I had nowhere to go, and I was so afraid! I ran from the tree to the backdoor of my human family's house. I cried and scratched on the door, desperate for a place away from the hard rain, thunder, and scary lightning.

After a few minutes, I realized my human family was not at home. I was on my own on the scariest night of my life.

I curled up in a ball, wishing it would all stop. I was wet, scared, and all alone. I wanted Sassy. I wanted my sisters. I wanted my *humans*!

While the rain was falling and the wind was blowing, things in the backyard started to blow around. The tricycle was blown up against the fence, and several toy balls went flying out of the yard. Leaves and tree branches were flying through the air. None of this was safe for a small dog. At any minute, something could hit me hard. But as I braced myself and laid low to the ground, thanks to God, nothing caused me to get hurt.

When the wind slowed down and the rain became soft, I relaxed a little and started to assess my situation. Surely, this was not how dogs were supposed to live? Aren't dogs created to love and be loved by humans? Aren't humans supposed to provide shelter, food, and water for their dogs in exchange for loyalty, love, and protection? What went wrong with my humans? What did I do wrong?

I started to think that something had to change in my situation. My fur was matted, the dirt and mud was collecting at a rapid rate, and now I had to endure the weather with no place to go. Maybe I needed to be more diligent in my job keeping the birds out of the backyard.

Surely if I showed my human family how hard I worked, they would at least provide me a shelter!

So I picked up the pace. If a bird came within inches of my yard, they got my ferocious bark and deep growl.

"Out of here! Stay out of my sight! Birds are not welcome!" I barked. I learned a really mean-sounding bark that would surely make any creature think twice before they bothered my human family.

My bark became unique, making a sound as I breathed in and a sound as I breathed out. I was a beast! I perfected the art of making the world take notice that I was a dog. "I might be small, but I will tear you apart if you get close to my yard!" (I would never have hurt anyone, but I sure wanted everyone to think that I would.)

Somehow, I was going to survive. I was determined that I would be loyal to my human family to the point of death. If the backyard was my domain, I would guard and protect it. I was a loyal dog.

CHAPTER 4

On My Own

A few weeks after the bad thunderstorm, I realized again that my human family was not home.

I depended on my humans to refill the water bowl and provide me with fresh dog food. It had been two days since I had heard a human moving around inside the house.

I had a water puddle in the yard from a recent rain, but it had been a couple of days with no food, and I was starting to get hungry. I looked around to see if there was something I could eat, but I had done my job so well, no creature would come close to my yard. There was nothing to catch and kill, so there was nothing to eat.

After the third day of no humans or food, I was desperate. I needed to find food! I looked out my fence and tried to see if other humans or dogs might be close enough to share some food with me.

Two houses down, I noticed a cat. I'm not too fond of cats, but they eat good food. I thought, *If I could just get out of my backyard and into the yard with the cat, maybe I could get something to eat. But how can I get out of my fence?*

I walked around and examined every flaw and weakness in the fence. I was thinking that maybe the bad storm might have weakened the fence somewhere that would allow me a chance to get out.

I noticed the fence was attached to the gate, which was a little higher with a gap underneath. This spot usually puddled with water, but now the water was drying up. I thought that this might be the best place of escape.

I started digging and digging under the gate until I had a little spot where I could push my head through. With all my force, I pushed my head and then body through the hole under the gate. I was out! I was out of my yard!

Now, I never intended to stay away for long, just long enough to steal the food from the cat and come right back to my human family. I was a loyal dog, and I loved my family. I knew I had a job to do in keeping the birds out of the yard. I would never abandon the humans. But when I got out of the yard, I became scared and started to run.

I do not know how far I traveled that first day, but I let my nose be my guide. My first stop was a big pile of trash. It must have been from a big family because it smelled good. Lots of food! Hamburger, French fries, and lots of ketchup! Boy, was it fun tearing through the wrappers and paper sacks to find the prize of a snack!

After I was full, I decided I needed to find some water. I looked around and noticed a puddle. I drank as much as I could. I needed to get back to my yard, but I could not remember which way was home. *Maybe after I rest I can find my way back,* I thought. I looked around and found a place under a bush to lie down. I fell fast asleep.

CHAPTER **5**

Missing My Humans

It didn't take many days of living on my own until I discovered that life without humans was not a pleasant prospect.

City streets did provide lots of places for shelter for a little dog. There were brick piles, garbage bins, bushes, and even an occasional shed, which protected me from the rain and heat. But they provided very little food and water and no love or attention.

As I pondered my situation, I remembered Sassy's words: "Dogs are happiest in the human world when they have a job to do to help the humans in their world." I remembered her telling me that one day that would be my ultimate desire. And here I was. Desiring a human family. I thought about my family and wished I could find my way back. I miss my yard, my job, and my humans.

Everywhere I went I couldn't find any humans who were interested in my situation. I would try to get close, but they would shoo me away. Just like I had scared off the birds from my backyard, humans scared me away to find a home someplace else.

One day while looking through a trash bin for food, I saw another dog. "This food is good!" I yelled. "There is more than I can eat. Come over here, and we can share!"

The dog seemed friendly and trotted over to my bin and helped me eat. He was a big brown dog with short hair and a long tail. "How long have you been on your own without humans?" I asked.

"Not long," he answered. "I live just down the street. I like to jump the fence every now and then to find out what is out here. I'm so glad I did today because this human food is good!"

"I cannot imagine ever jumping a fence just to explore the world. I dug out of my yard because I was hungry and needed to find food. Now I cannot find my way back. Do you think you might help me find my home?" I asked.

"I don't know any areas of Lubbock except here. I never go far. After I eat this food, I will go back to my house and wait for my humans to let me back into the yard. If you like, you can go back with me. Maybe my humans will take you in."

I followed the big brown dog to his house, but when we arrived, his family would not let me in the yard. They swooshed me away with a stick and yelled, "Get away! Get away!"

I don't blame them. I looked terrible with all the mud and matted fur. What was I to do?

The occasional trash can with food seemed to be farther and farther away. I sometimes went three or four days without anything to eat. My stomach growled. I was very hungry!

At night sometimes I would dream of Sassy and how wonderful life was with her. I was sure by now she had had more puppies and was being the same good mom to them as she was to me. Oh, how I wished I had a good human home. Even if I had just one person to love, I would have loved him or her with all my heart.

The Kind Man 6

My circumstance on the street was teaching me that not every human was kind. How was I to tell which human might want a dog and which might get a stick and swoosh me away?

One night while I was looking through the trash for food, a man came out of a house and saw me. He must have felt sad for me because he gave me a look that looked gentle and kind. He started talking softly to me. "Hi, little one. What are you doing? Are you hungry? Look here. I have some bread for you!"

I noticed he had some food in his hand. I was very hungry, so I decided to try to see what this human was all about. I slowly walked toward him.

He let me eat the food, and then he opened the door to his garage. He motioned for me to go inside. "Go on in, little doggy. It will be a good place for you to sleep tonight."

I lowered my head, tucked in my tail, and accepted his offer of a roof over my head and entered the garage.

This small area smelled like a leaky car. Looking around, I saw a car like the one I had ridden in to live with my human family. I did not want to go near it. I knew it could go fast!

As I sat there looking at the car, the man came closer and bent down to pick me up. I stepped back and gave a small growl. Not much, but just enough to let the man know that I never wanted to be picked up!

"That's okay, little one," he said. "I am not going to touch you if you don't want me to."

Just to be on the safe side, I gave him one last little bark.

The man left the garage and went through a door and into the house. I could smell food from the other side of the door, but it was obvious that the man intended for me to stay out by the car.

I looked around this area and noticed a towel. It smelled like the car, but it looked comfortable enough that I might use it to curl up and take a nap.

After a few minutes of resting, the door opened and the man appeared again. This time he had two bowls, one with food and one with water. Boy, did that food smell good!

"Thank you, thank you!" I yelped. I jumped up and down and wagged my tail as a big thank you. Unlike my human mom, this man didn't yell at my joy. Instead, he laughed and turned to walk back into the house. "There you go, little one. Eat and drink all you like. You sleep here tonight, and in the morning, we will decide if we can find you a permanent home."

I didn't reply. I just started eating. It had been a long time since I had a full meal and water to drink. I felt so satisfied that I laid down on the cool floor and fell fast asleep.

CHAPTER 7

The Pound

I woke the next morning to the sound of two men talking. It startled me at first because I forgot where I was, but I quickly remembered that I was in the garage.

The men were talking about a dog in the garage. I heard them say, "This poor dog needs a real human home." I jumped up and down. Yes! Yes! I needed a new human home! Maybe it was here! In this garage!

The two men came to the garage door. Thinking positive thoughts, I tried not to be afraid, but I soon noticed that one had a large pole with a net on the end. I realized I was trapped in this garage with no way out. I started barking and growling. I became very afraid. I barked and growled and ran around, but the two men were too much for me. With a big swipe of the net, I was caught.

When a dog is caught, it has a choice: bite or submit. I chose to submit. I laid back my ears, tucked in my tail, and shut up. I knew my fate was in this human's hands. I could only wait and see. Was he kind? Was he mean?

The second man had a big truck with a crate for dogs in the back. He took me from the garage to this crate.

I could smell the crates, and my nose told me lots of dogs and cats had been in them. The overwhelming smell added to my fear.

"Thanks for calling the pound," I heard the second man say. "It is not good for a dog to be out on the streets alone. I can tell this little one is tired and hungry. We will try to find a good home for her as soon as possible. For now, I will take her to the city animal shelter for evaluation."

I looked back at the kind man and the garage. "Bye, little one," he said. "I hope you have a good life with your new family."

Those kind words relaxed me for the short ride to the city animal shelter, also known as the pound. There they transferred me to a special holding crate surrounded by more dogs than I had ever seen before.

There were all kinds: big dogs, little dogs; dogs with short hair, dogs with long hair; brown dogs, black dogs, white dogs, and spotted dogs; dogs that were barking, dogs that were sleeping. They were all mixed up!

My new crate had a water bowl, food bowl, and a blanket. At least here it looked like I was not going to be hungry, thirsty, cold, or wet.

CHAPTER 8

Meeting Coal

The pound collected animals from the entire city. Sometimes the animals were lost. Sometimes the human family did not want the animal anymore. Sometimes the human family abandoned them. One thing was sure; there were too many animals at the pound. There would not be enough human families to take all the dogs. The humans at the pound had to examine each new dog and decide which was best to live in the human world.

When the dog catcher caught me, I was a mess. Not only was my fur matted with mud, I was very skinny and looked sickly. My eyes must have had a wild, scared look. So it did not surprise me when the pound decided I was not the best prospect for a new human family. I was placed in an area of unwanted dogs to wait and see what would happen next.

I can't say I was happy about this dim outlook, but at least in the pound I had the joy of other animals around me and a full stomach.

In the crate next to me was a big black Lab.

"Hi, my name is Corkey. What is yours?" I asked.

"Coal," answered the Lab. "What you in for, Corkey?"

I wasn't really sure how to answer that one, so I had to think. "I guess I'm in here because I ran away from my human family. I was hungry and thirsty and thought I was alone, so I made my escape and lived on the streets for several months. I found out I really do not like living on the streets. It is lonely, and I was hungry all the time."

"Understand your problem there. I have never lived on the streets or been on my own, but Ralph the beagle over across the way told me all about it. I really never wanted to be without my humans," answered Coal.

Coal continued to tell me that he had lived with a family for over ten years. His humans had to move into a smaller house and could not have such a big dog, so he was sent to the pound. Once at the pound, it seemed no one wanted to take home an older dog, so he was sent to the undesirable area like me.

After all the excitement, I decided to rest. I curled up and fell asleep, dreaming of what I might be if I could have a forever human family. When I woke up, I felt a new determination that maybe there really was hope of a good future for me.

That night, I dreamed I talked with God.

"God, why is life so hard for little dogs like me?" I asked.

"Little one, I did not create you for a hard life. I created you to be a help to the human world. Dogs have always remained true to that purpose and place in the world, but humans have many times disregarded this purpose.

"Humans were created by Me to take care of the animal kingdom and the earth. I made them special to communicate with Me. Humans left that natural order and started living their lives selfishly without acknowledging Me or My plan.

"Many humans refuse to notice I even exist," God continued. "The peace and love I have for them has long since been forgotten, and because they do not listen to my natural order of things, animals suffer."

I woke up from the dream realizing that I was a perfect dog. God was taking care of me; I just needed to keep hoping that things could change.

I looked over and noticed that Coal was awake.

"Coal, is there no hope? Do humans never come in here to take us to a forever home?"

"Well, there is a little hope. Once a month, a group from an animal foundation visits the pound. They are given money to help rescue dogs that have no hope. The name of this group is McCoy Animal Rescue. Jessie is a real kind lady in charge of this group. They have been by to look at me several times.

"There is not much hope in them choosing you, however. If they do not want me, what makes you think they would take a skinny, dirty dog like you?"

"When is Jessie due back again?" I asked.

"It should be soon," Coal replied. "But you never know."

CHAPTER 9

The Rescue

"Coal, how long will they keep a dog here in this area? And what happens if a human family never comes?"

"Well, I didn't want to alarm you further, but the rest is bad news. I really think you might be better off believing there is a little hope than knowing how bad it could get," Coal reluctantly replied.

I thought about it for a minute and decided that I liked to know what was coming next, if I could.

"Give me the bad news. I'm ready now to know the whole truth of what might happen to me next." I spoke with a quiet resolve and then lay down.

Coal did not know for sure what might happen next, but the rumor was that if a dog could not go to a forever human

43

family, he or she would be given some medicine that would make him or her go to sleep and never wake up again.

"Oh no!" I exclaimed. "Surely not! I will just have to believe that there is someone out there somewhere who would just love a good, loyal, bird-chasing dog like me!"

Now I was worried again. I had to think a lot about what could I do to make sure a human liked me. What were my options? I was not sure.

Days passed, and I felt stronger with my food and water. But I was still tired and slept a lot.

One day, while asleep, I heard a commotion. Soon all the dogs in the pound were barking.

"Over here!" they barked. "Pick me! Pick me!"

I looked over at Coal. He was jumping in his crate, barking the loudest. "It's Jessie from McCoy's!" Coal bellowed. "Show her you are alive and have energy! This is your only hope!"

Hmm, I thought to myself. *I can see that all this barking and yelping is getting everyone a longer stay in the pound. I think I will just lay here and pretend to sleep through the commotion.*

As Jessie toured the pound, she walked up and down the aisles and looked into the crates. "I'm looking for dogs with the best attitude and that do not look sick," she said.

As you can guess, I was not on top of her list.

When Jessie walked by my crate, she peered in and said, "Holly! Is that you, Holly?" I looked up at her with wide eyes.

Why are you looking for Holly? I'm Corky, I thought to myself.

Jessie looked at me and cried, "No, she is not Holly. My Holly is gone. Poor dog. She is so dirty and thin. So sad." She shook her head and walked away.

My chance was over. I looked sad and unsure. I was trying to play it calm and cool, not like the other dogs that were jumping and yelping. But it did not work. Jessie passed me by.

I laid back down on my bed, closed my eyes, and tried not to think about losing my chance of rescue so fast.

The other dogs were barking so much that the noise was giving me a headache. I turned my back to the others and tried to think.

"Hey you," I heard someone say. I looked up and was so surprised to see Jessie looking in at me through the crate bars. "Want a treat?"

"Sure," I replied, turning to face my hope.

Jessie opened the crate and offered me the treat, which I took and immediately hid under my blanket for later. She laughed and said, "She's such a mess, but I can tell she's gentle of spirit. She looks so much like my old dog, Holly. I loved Holly so much that I think, in her memory, I will take this dog with me and try to help her find a human home."

My thoughts went crazy! I had been passed over all my life for the more beautiful Maltese. But this time, my looks were wanted! I looked like Holly! I had the right look after all! My black and white, wild, thin fur was the very thing that had rescued me from possible death!

Jessie gathered me up and took me to her rescue shelter. The first thing she did was give me my very first shower. I had never had a bath let alone a shower. It was so scary—it was like rain but not cold. I laid my ears as far back as I could and put my tail between my legs. Jessie tried to be gentle, but she had lots of mud and matting to get out of my fur. All that washing and combing really hurt!

"I am sorry this hurts you, Holly. You will never find a forever human family if you are not clean," Jessie said as she dried me off. "You are such a cute little dog without all that mud. You are very good-natured to have endured that shower. I think someone will like you very much."

After all the grooming, Jessie took me to my new crate. It was bigger than the one at the pound. There were several dogs in other crates around me. I had a blanket, food, and water, and now all I wanted to do was rest. Clean and relieved to have the mud out of my fur, I felt better than I had since my days with Sassy.

Across the hall was a little Pomeranian.

"Hi, I'm Corky … I mean, Holly. Can you tell me what life is like here? I'm a little scared and not sure what is going to happen next."

"Sure, Holly," replied the Pomeranian. "My name is Polly. I have been here for several months now, and I can show you all the ropes. This is a safe place where you will get all the food and water you need. It is fun living here with the other dogs around, and the humans who come in and talk to us are all very nice."

"I have had many experiences in my short life. And I have come through them all. That shower I had last night was real scary, but now I feel so good and clean, I can see it was well worth the fright!" I answered assuredly.

"Yes, I agree. The shower is good. My fur is about the same length as yours, so I imagine your shower was as painful as mine," Polly replied. "The next thing that will happen to you is quite scary too. I want to tell you what is going to happen so you won't be scared like I was."

"Thanks so much! I'm almost afraid to find out what's next, but I will listen." I lay closer to hear.

"Every dog that comes to this rescue must be fixed so as to not ever have any puppies. This will help control the dog population. If there are too many dogs and not enough humans to take care of them, the dogs will suffer. Making sure dogs do not have puppies is how humans help keep there from becoming too many dogs to care for in the future."

The Pomeranian continued. "In order for a dog not have puppies, he or she must have surgery. You will have to go to an animal hospital and have an animal doctor do surgery. The animal doctor is called a Veterinarian, or Vet for short."

"Wow!" I said.

"For boy dogs, they remove their testicles. This is called neutering. For girl dogs, they remove their womb. This is called spaying."

"What's a womb?" I asked.

"The womb is an organ inside your body. It is the place where puppies live inside their mother until they are born," Polly explained.

I thought about this. "You know, I never thought about having puppies. My mom's job was having puppies, but my job was chasing birds. I guess having puppies would keep me from being a good bird chaser," I replied. "I guess I need to get myself prepared for surgery!"

"One more thing. Get ready for many shots."

"Shots? What are shots?" I asked.

"They are small plastic tubes with needles on the end. The Vet puts the needles in your leg to give you medicine to make you strong and to keep you from getting sick," Polly answered.

"Does it hurt?" I asked.

"Only a little. Really not much."

"Thanks for the heads-up. Knowing what is going to happen gives me time to prepare." This answer made me seem sure, but it was a brave front. I really was scared.

The next morning, Jessie came to my crate. She put a leash around my neck and led me to her car. It was time to go to the Vet.

When we arrived at the Vet's office, the Vet took me into the surgery room. I was very scared!

There was lots of noise and bright lights. I wasn't sure what they were going to do to me, and I didn't want it to hurt! All I could do was pray, "God, help me be strong. Help me be brave."

I don't remember too much about the spaying or the shots. They gave me some medicine to make me sleep, and when I woke up, I was back at the rescue, lying on my blanket. I had a little pain in my stomach, so I decided it might be best to just lay still. I curled up on my bed and fell back asleep.

CHAPTER **10**

Ms. Becky

While I was asleep, I heard the sweetest voice I had ever heard. It was a woman. She was as round as she was tall. She was real fat! She had white hair and a huge smile to go with her soft words. She opened my crate and handed me a treat. Even though I didn't feel too good, my instincts told me she was kind, so I accepted the treat, buried it in my blanket for later, and laid back down as I listened to the woman and Jessie talk.

"I think I like the Pomeranian the best," said the woman. "I like this black and white dog, but the Pomeranian looks healthier."

"Yes, the Pomeranian is a better choice, but I have promised her to someone," Jessie said. "You will have to wait a few days to see if they come and get her if you think you want the Pomeranian."

The woman thought about it a bit longer and then came back to my crate and gave me a pat on the top of my head. I was glad she didn't try to pick me up or she would have heard my growl! I just lay there, trying not to be afraid.

"I'll take this one," the woman said, pointing at me.

"Good choice," Jessie replied. "I will just have to fill out the paperwork and she is yours!"

While waiting for the paperwork, the woman sat down to talk to me. "My name is Ms. Becky. I am going to take you home to your new forever human family!"

Was she really going to take me home? I perked up—but not too much. I did not want to show too much excitement—just enough to let Ms. Becky know it was okay with me.

I didn't know for sure if this was a good human or a bad human. All I knew was she seemed gentle. It wasn't long before I was in the car next to her, riding to only God knew where to my new home.

"You are going to live with me at my house," she said. "I live in Levelland, out in the country. You will be able to run and play, but I plan on you staying inside with me. My boys are grown, and my husband works out of town. You will be my new best four-legged friend!"

What? I thought. *Does this lady want a friend? Did I hear her say I was living in a house? Not outside?* Could I have such hope that this was a kind human home and I would love being her dog? "I sure hope this is the best place for me," I prayed to myself. *"I need to just be quiet, try to stay calm, and see what is next."*

CHAPTER 11

My Levelland Home

Ms. Becky was right; it was a pretty place. There were a few trees and lots of grass. I could smell the cotton growing across the road and could sense that Ms. Becky was as cautious around me as I was around her. She didn't push me to get out of the car. She just opened the car door and let me jump down myself. Then she opened the door to her house and let me walk inside.

It was a small house but big enough for me. Ms. Becky had decorations on all the walls with chairs and sofas and tables and rugs everywhere! What a place to explore!

It seemed like there was furniture in every spot. I could hide under tables or behind chairs or jump on the sofa. There were white lacy table coverings on some of the furniture, and stacked around were books, papers, glass figures, and stuff I had never seen before.

There were many wires going to wall plugs. These wires went to the TV, a radio, a computer, and many lamps. The floor had carpet and rugs that held lots of smells, so I immediately started to sniff around and explore with my nose.

Ms. Becky showed me where the water and food bowls were, and then she showed me a crate with a dog bed inside. I continued to sniff and smell until I felt comfortable that there were no more animals in the house—just me.

Ms. Becky went about her chores in the house, singing softly and talking to me. "You are going to love it here. I sure have been lonely since my last pet went to glory." I wondered, *What is glory? Was it another shelter?*

When it was bedtime, I wondered what I was supposed to do. Ms. Becky walked into her bedroom, and I followed close behind her.

"It is time for bed now," she said. She looked at me and patted the side of the bed.

I looked up at her shyly, gave a quick jump, and landed on the bed.

Ms. Becky gently reached and lightly patted my head. Her movements were slow and on purpose. I responded to her touch with a light lick of her hand. This was when I started to think that life with Ms. Becky just might be okay.

Ms. Becky pulled back the blanket on the bed, climbed in, and laid her head on the pillow. I had never been on a human bed before. *Is this where humans sleep?* I thought. *Am I supposed to sleep here?*

Apparently so. Ms. Becky turned out the lights, and I laid down.

That first night I was afraid to sleep, but I was also afraid to move. I just didn't know about Ms. Becky, this new bed, or this new life.

The next morning, Ms. Becky took me outside. We walked around and looked at the grass. I needed to potty, but what if Ms. Becky didn't like it? What if I didn't find the right spot? So I decided to hold it. No need to start trouble if I can hold it!

I kept sniffing and waiting until I noticed Ms. Becky turn her back to me. I hurried and went potty. She turned around just as I finished, and I got scared. *Will she be mad?* I wondered.

"Good job! I am so proud of you for pottying outside. Come back in. I have a treat for you," she replied with a gentle voice as she opened the back door.

Whew! She is not mad! I thought to myself.

I walked in and waited for Ms. Becky, who reached for a doggy treat that smelled like bacon and gave it to me. Wow, did that taste good!

The rest of the day, Ms. Becky watched my behavior. Every time I started sniffing the rugs, acting like I needed to potty, Ms. Becky opened the door and let me go outside and sniff just the right spot in the grass. Ms. Becky always gave me a treat when I came back into the house.

I quickly learned that if I pottied outside in the grass and hurried back inside to Ms. Becky, I would get a treat. This might be a good home after all!

While Ms. Becky sat in her favorite chair, I stayed across the room. I had been use to humans shooing me, so I never wanted a human to pick me up. It seemed Ms. Becky wanted me to sit with her in the chair, but I was wary.

She began to speak gently. "Come here, little one. Come sit with me and watch TV." After a little assurance of her patting the arm of the chair, I slowly walked closer, sitting and waiting every few inches to be sure I was doing what she wanted. Finally, I reached the chair, sprang up beside her, and braced myself in case she decided to throw me off.

But to my surprise, she smiled and began stroking my fur. "You have the softest fur. It looks real wild and coarse, but it isn't. You aren't anything like you look. You are gentle and soft. I can tell you have had a hard time, but don't you worry. You are safe here, and we have a lifetime to get to know each other. Just sit here beside me and be my friend."

As she talked, I learned that Ms. Becky was trying to give me a new name. She wanted to name me something unique for my unique look.

"I need to call my husband," she said. "He works a long way off in Russia."

As she talked into the phone, she said, "I want to name her Sweet Pea because she is so sweet, but I also want to name her something strong to go with her looks. She has black pointed ears, a cute white short nose, and is spotted all over."

Ms. Becky continued. "She is unique. She does not look like any other dog. She is some kind of strange mix, but cute as a button!"

Then after a short minute of silence, I heard her say, "Sobaka! That's it! I love the name Sobaka! But what does Sobaka mean? Dog in Russian?"

That's right. That is how I got my new name. My name became Sobaka, which means "dog" in Russian. After all this time, my new name is *Dog*!

CHAPTER 12

Kennel Cough

The third night in my new home, we started with our regular bedtime routine. Ms. Becky put me up on her bed, climbed in beside me, and started petting me. She was talking gently, trying to make me feel at home. But I was starting to feel sick.

I had never been sick before, so I wasn't sure what to do. I had the strong urge to cough, but I didn't want Ms. Becky to know. I tried to hold it, hold it, hold it … but out it came! A cough, another, and then another.

It hurt deep down inside my body. I started to feel hot. I was sick.

Ms. Becky sat up in bed and patted my head. She looked very worried. She knew I was sick. All night I coughed, and

Ms. Becky petted me and cried. I heard her praying, "God, help Sobaka. She is your creation. Sobaka needs Your help."

This human prayer sounded so gentle and sweet, and God's presence seemed so real. This human did not forget God. This human followed her instincts to care about me! I finally found a human who loved me and followed the instincts God had given her. I was designed to be her four-legged, bird-chasing friend, but right now I was sick.

The next morning, Ms. Becky took me to the Vet. I was scared. It had been less than a week since my last visit to the Vet when I had had the surgery and all kinds of shots. But this time I was sick. As the Vet talked to Ms. Becky, I found out that I had developed kennel cough.

The Vet said, "Kennel cough is a disease dogs catch when they are around a lot of different dogs with lots of different germs and illnesses. Kennel cough is like a cold for humans, but it can be deadly for dogs."

The Vet gave Ms. Becky medicine for me and told her that I might not make it. Ms. Becky started to cry. I had only been with her for three days and it appeared that she already loved me. Her face looked broken.

Once back home, Ms. Becky let me stay in her bed. She gave me the medicine, patted my head, held me, and prayed. I don't know how I survived, but I am here today. Those days when I had the high fever and the terrible cough gave me a chance to find out that Ms. Becky was real kind and loving. I had a wonderful home.

As the days went by, I got stronger and better, and Ms. Becky started teaching me the way of humans. Slowly, I learned to always potty outside, to come when she called my name, to sit in the chair with her, to go into the crate when she was gone, and to play in my new surroundings. Ms. Becky and I had everything figured out accept one thing: I needed a job!

CHAPTER

My New Job 13

Every dog needs a job. He or she needs something to do to help the humans. God designed dogs with the desire to be loyal, loving, and protective and to serve the humans with a job.

I was having a hard time trying to decide what kind of work Ms. Becky needed. I couldn't chase birds because there were no birds inside the house. I didn't notice any mice or bugs. *What could I do to help my human family?*

My Levelland house was in the country. It sat on a quiet street with very few cars or noises. The neighbors were a long way away, so I didn't notice other people or pets. Usually dogs will chase or bark, but there was nothing to chase and there was nothing to bark at or about. What could be my new job?

One day, I heard a sound like a car coming up the drive. I started barking right away. Ms. Becky heard me barking and went to look out the window.

"Sobaka, someone is coming to see me! You let me know someone was driving up the drive! Good job!"

Soon after the car noise, I heard *ding-dong*. Somebody was ringing the doorbell. I continued barking and growling, barking and growling. I was using the ferocious sound I had learned from chasing birds out of my old yard.

Ms. Becky opened the door and talked with a man standing outside. I stood beside her, ready to pounce if this man seemed to cause Ms. Becky any harm.

After the man left, Ms. Becky said, "You were such a good dog, Sobaka! You alerted me that I had a visitor. And you let the visitor know that I had a dog and he had better beware! I think that deserves a treat!" I got a delicious doggy treat. I now had a job! If I heard a car come close to the house, I would jump up, bark, and growl. This alerted Ms. Becky that someone was coming. She seemed so happy, and I was so proud!

One night, Ms. Becky and I were asleep when I heard a noise. I didn't know what it was, but my instincts told me something was not right.

I started barking and growling and ran to the backdoor, where I heard the sound. It scared Ms. Becky because she was asleep and had not heard the noise. She jumped up from bed, grabbed her gun from the closet, and started walking toward the door. "Who is out there?" she shouted. No one answered.

We both stood still as we listened for any sign of trouble. I was alert, and Ms. Becky was watching and listening.

After a few of minutes of silence, Ms. Becky walked through the house and checked all the doors and windows to make sure they were locked. We were safe. Everything seemed in place, and all was still locked.

It appeared that whatever or whoever had made the noise was now gone. I realized I must have scared an intruder away with my wonderful bark.

After putting the gun away, Ms. Becky gave me a hug. I was so happy. I had let Ms. Becky know there was danger and had scared off anyone who might have wanted to harm her with my ferocious growl.

My skill of mean barking was a good thing and was just what Ms. Becky needed from her four-legged friend.

Forever Home 14

Ms. Becky and I settled into a routine. I would follow her from room to room as she did her chores each day. When she was cooking, I would sit alert at her feet, waiting until she dropped a morsel of food. In a way, I was a broom for Ms. Becky because I kept the floor clean!

Ms. Becky loved to play the piano. At first the loud noise coming out of the big wooden box scared me, but Ms. Becky loved the piano and played it often. I had a choice to make: either be near Ms. Becky or stay in another room while she played the piano. I decided I would rather sit with Ms. Becky. So I learned to sit under her stool while she played.

I didn't just follow Ms. Becky around the house; sometimes, I got to run errands with her. This was absolutely the best part of my day when I got to go! It didn't matter where. Anywhere was great!

I learned to watch closely and noticed that if Ms. Becky put on her shoes, it meant she was leaving the house. As soon as she picked up those shoes, I would look at her with excitement.

"Am I going today? Do I get to go?" I asked with my tail wagging and jumping up and down.

At this point, Ms. Becky would decide if I could go or if I had to stay home. I listened closely, ears alert. If she said yes, I knew I was going in the car. If she said no, I was going to stay home. Which was it today?

"Today you can go," Ms. Becky replied.

"Yea! Yea!" I answered with cheer. I was getting to go and it meant I could ride in the car!

I didn't like riding in the car when I first came to Ms. Becky's house. I had had many bad experiences going places that I really didn't want to go, feeling like I was being tossed around, and not being able to see where I was going. But Ms. Becky fixed a bed for me in the front seat, right next to her on the center console. I would sit and watch the world go by faster than any dog could ever run!

Thinking back to the first time I saw a car while living with Sassy, I thought cars were scary. I laugh now because cars can be fun. I am still afraid of cars when I am outside, but riding inside one is a great treat!

Continuing to remember my life with Sassy, I realized it had been one year since I was born. What a year!

Looking back on my life before Ms. Becky, I realized that living with Sassy taught me what makes a good dog. Living with my first human family taught me what makes a good human family. And living on the streets alone taught me that I need humans in my life. Now, living with Ms. Becky teaches us both that we need each other.

All the experiences of my life had molded me into the perfect dog. Looking back, I remember my prayer before I left Sassy: "God, You know my desire is to be with a human family that will teach me to develop into a loyal, loving, hardworking dog. Please send a family to me that I can call my own. Help me to be that special dog to a special human."

It seemed at the time that my prayers were not answered, but now I see that all the things in my life helped me to become that loyal, loving, hardworking dog.

All throughout my life, I was never picked first. Ms. Becky didn't pick me first. Jessie didn't pick me first. The first human family didn't pick me first. But in the end, I was the best choice.

Yes, I have had a good life. I plan on living many, many more years. I will have many more stories to tell about this wonderful thing between humans and dogs. And I will have a good life!

About the Author

Becky Williams is a Christian minister with a love for pets. Her desire in writing this book is to give the reader insight into the worries a pet might have in the care of different human families. The author also wishes for the reader to understand that dogs, like humans, have an understanding of God as their creator and provider.